The Girl from the Northern Mountains

Written and Illustrated by Lois Furtado

AuthorHouse™
1663 Liberty Drive
Bloomington, IN 47403
www.authorhouse.com
Phone: 1 (800) 839-8640

Because of the dynamic nature of the Internet, any web addresses or links contained in this book may have changed since publication and may no longer be valid. The views expressed in this work are solely those of the author and do not necessarily reflect the views of the publisher, and the publisher hereby disclaims any responsibility for them.

Any people depicted in stock imagery provided by Getty Images are models, and such images are being used for illustrative purposes only.
Certain stock imagery © Getty Images.

Scripture quotations marked NIV are taken from the Holy Bible, New International Version®. NIV®. Copyright © 1973, 1978, 1984 by International Bible Society. Used by permission of Zondervan. All rights reserved. [Biblica]

This book is printed on acid-free paper.

ISBN: 978-1-7283-4028-9 (sc)
ISBN: 978-1-7283-4027-2 (e)

Library of Congress Control Number: 2019920926

Print information available on the last page.

Published by AuthorHouse 01/03/2020

authorHOUSE

This book is dedicated to "third-culture kids."

"But our citizenship is in heaven. And we eagerly await a Savior from there, the Lord Jesus Christ" ~ Philippians 3:20 (NIV)

Foreword

By Julia Levy

Most people have heard the first stanza of the serenity prayer: "God, give me the grace to accept with serenity the things that cannot be changed, the courage to change the things which should be changed, and the wisdom to know the difference." In *The Girl from the Northern Mountains*, my friend Lois Furtado has shared through allegory her heart-wrenching, personal journey of learning how to live out the second, lesser known and perhaps more demanding stanza:

> "Living one day at a time, enjoying one moment at a time, *accepting hardship as a pathway to peace, taking, as Jesus did, this sinful world as it is, not as I would have it*, Trusting that You will make all things right, If I surrender to Your will, So that I may be reasonably happy in this life, And supremely happy with You forever in the next. Amen."

This story, which began as a graduate school assignment, challenging students to share their cross-cultural experiences, quickly became a much deeper project of reflection and healing for Lois. Illustrated through the eyes of her inner child, she revisits the events and feelings of her past, embracing the messy work of baring her heart on her sleeve. In doing so, she comes to terms with that most difficult line of the serenity prayer: "taking this sinful world as it is, not as I would have it."

At the age of sixteen, Lois moved with her family from a small, working-class town in northern England to the cultural melting pot that is south Florida. Here *The Girl from the Northern Mountains* finds its beginning. Written for third-culture kids who so often struggle with their sense of identity and belonging, "The Girl" is intentionally left nameless. Her name belongs to the readers, the ones who need to know that they aren't without a people in the wide world that they've traversed. One of their kinsmen even wrote a story about them.

But *The Girl From the Northern Mountains* isn't just about the turmoil of immigrating as a child. It's also and emphatically a story about the inescapable vulnerability of being human, and the choice with which we are all faced: to love and feel pain, or to keep oneself at a safe distance from others and feel nothing.

In the end, The Girl chooses to love, which is to say, she chooses a life of breaking. She learns to ask God for the grace to accept a world of jagged-edged, baggage-carrying people as they are and not as she would have them.

As you read this lovely story about the reality of being human, do yourself the favor of inviting your inner child along for a listen. Let her or him get lost in the pictures, interrupt with a dozen questions, laugh, cry, even get distracted by their own daydreaming. Spend time with her and know that you are whole when you are together.

The Girl from the Northern Mountains

Written and Illustrated by Lois Furtado

Along time ago there was a place in the far-out Northern Seas called the Island of Monarchs. It was a cold and damp island, but the hearts of the island people created a warmth in the weather through their exceptional friendliness. It was the warmth of their hearts that released warm air into the atmosphere, which allowed the climate to be very comfortable for everyone. The people of the island were known to be the most sincere and hospitable of citizens.

In the North of the island, there were tall stony mountains. Oddly enough, the farther a person would go up North into the mountains, the warmer the temperature would become. How can this strange phenomenon be, you may ask? This is because to live up in the heights of the mountains, the bigger the person's heart needed to be to survive. Simply put, bigger hearts created more warmth in the air. The big hearts of the Northern people created many lovely sunny days for all those who resided in the Northern Mountains.

There was a slightly chubby little girl, with crooked teeth and an unfamiliar Twinkle in her eye who resided in the Northern Mountains. She loved her island and its people. Even though the girl faintly recognized her physical imperfections, she did not concentrate on them too much because her desire to experience delightful things naturally denied her to focus on such boring issues. Besides, her favorite thing to do was dance and make new friends along the way. Her slight chubbiness and crooked smile didn't seem to affect those ambitions. The little girl greeted every stranger with confidence, "Hi, will you be my friend?" The girl found this approach to be most effective. She did indeed find many friends!

With such lovely weather in the Northern Mountains, one might wonder why didn't every islander want to live up there, or why would Northerners desire to live in the Southern Lowlands? You see, the journey to and from the Northern Mountains was incredibly difficult. The paths were steep and dangerous. It was known as a hazardous and an uncertain journey. Families who had been settled in the Northern Mountains for hundreds of years would retell fearful tales of death and loss of the brave sojourners who attempted it. Besides, many of the Southerners were used to the colder climate and they lost their desire for warmer weather because they found the North slightly suffocating.

Although the Northern Mountain tribe were very kindhearted and accepting of those few brave people that made it up the mountain, they were not so accepting towards their own who wanted to go down the mountain. The tribe would celebrate as each new brave member joined the Northern Mountains. Nevertheless, there was one thing they were very uncomfortable with and didn't celebrate well: The Twinkle.

What is a Twinkle? Twinkles are rare in the Northern Mountains and they are found in people's eyes. The Twinkle reflects the Starlight, which shines brightly from the Eternal Land. The Starlight never stops shining, and those children who receive this Twinkle - their eyes get brighter as they grow older. Because the Twinkle was not of a natural inheritance from the Northern Mountains, it caused fear in the rest of the tribe. They feared that the Twinkle would challenge their tribal hearts, and in turn, possibly lose their warmth that produced lovely sunny days that they all enjoyed so much. The problem was also that the Twinkle would tend to shine too brightly on nights or in dark corners. The light that the Twinkle produced, annoyed the tribe because it had the habit of exposing certain activities that they would like to keep secret. And this is when things became difficult for the little girl, because she was one of those rare Northerners who inherited the Twinkle from the Starlight.

At first, the slightly chubby little girl, with the crooked smile, and an unfamiliar Twinkle in her eye, didn't feel much different from the rest of her tribe. She loved her people. She enjoyed dancing with her tribe the most and truly had a deep desire to be sincere friends with everyone in the

Northern Mountains. For quite a while, she was able to partake of most Northern rituals without her eyes shining too brightly onto others. But as she got a little older, it became increasingly more difficult to do so. Because of her Twinkle, she started to lose friends, which created a deep sense of insecurity. Many didn't understand her Twinkle, and other parents would teach her friends stories of mockery about those who had inherited it. As a result, she became a target for bullying, which led the girl to experience loneliness for the very first time.

One time there was a great big party that the whole tribe was planning. It was the talk of the town for many days. Everyone received an invitation – that is everyone but the little girl. Her fear of being lonely and not having many friends, quickly became a real threat to her young life. The night of the party arrived, but she never received an invitation. So, with deep sadness, she stayed home in her pajamas and slowly waited for the night to pass by. As she was settling in, to her surprise, there was a knock at her door. "Who can that be, she thought?" It was her friends! She answered her door in her pajamas, and to her disbelief they stated, "We feel so bad that you were not invited to the event. We want you to join us! Why don't you get changed into your party clothes, and come join the party?" With sheer delight (and slight puzzlement), she didn't think twice and quickly got changed and joined her friends. The girl was so happy to hear that it was all a mix up, and that she was wanted. As she was walking to the party with her friends, she got to the event and her friends started acting strangely. They started whispering and laughing. They were almost at the entrance of the event and her friends turned around and said to the little girl, "We were only joking" they started sniggering to one another. They continued, "You are not really invited. We just wanted to tease you, and it looks like it worked!" Sheer embarrassment and humiliation rushed through the little girl's body. She wanted to hide her tears, but there was so much emotion she felt like she was going to explode. Tears ran down her chubby cheeks. She ran all the way home, alone and ashamed. This girl who had anxiously wanted to be friends with everyone became quite sad and disconnected, to the point where her desire to dance had diminished.

One night, the little girl's father had a dream directly from the Starlight who lived in the Eternal Land. The Starlight revealed to him that he had to take his family to the Newlands, where there was more freedom for those who were born with a Twinkle and there was much meaningful work for him and his family to do there. The whole family had received the Twinkle gene, and it was getting more uncomfortable to stay in the familiarity of the warm Northern Mountains.

After he awoke, the father expressed his desire to relocate to the Newlands where the family's Twinkle would be more accepted and exciting work was being pre-arranged for them. The family had to combat all the natural fears that were attached to the dangers of going down the mountain and grieving the potential loss about the warm climate that they were so accustomed to. Other tribal members retold the fearful fables of danger to the family, hoping that they would truly understand the risks, and perhaps change their minds of the ridiculous idea of leaving the Northern Mountains. Even though the family (including the girl's two older brothers) had genuine fears about coming down the mountain and leaving the Island of Monarchs, the fear of not following the Starlight was graver. The father looked deeply into his little girl's Twinkled eyes and said, "Your future is in the Newlands, darling. You can bring the warmth of the Northern Mountains with you and share it with all the new friends you'll make. Perhaps, you'll find new reasons to dance."

Even though the tribe didn't truly understand the family's motives for leaving the Northern Mountains, the tribe eventually gave kind parting words. With mixed emotions, they said their difficult goodbyes and began their journey.

The mountains were indeed dangerous and challenging. The steeper the journey became, the more often her mother glanced back up in nostalgia to the Northern Mountains. However, what made the journey down the mountains bearable, was that they packed light. That had heard that most people's deadly mistake was to attempt to go up and down the mountains with lots of personal baggage. The only thing the family brought were a few essentials, some photographs, and the little girl brought her special family heirloom that her grandmother gave to her. The heirloom was given so that the little girl would never forget the warmth of the mountains of her childhood home. It was the most beautiful necklace with a big clear blue stone that reminded her of how the sky kissed the top of the Northern Mountains.

When the night was closing in, the family remembered stories they were told about when most accidents occurred - in the dark. Well, the most remarkable thing happened! Suddenly, their Twinkles in their eyes shined as bright as a lighthouse. Never had they seen their Twinkles shine so brilliantly. It became a natural light onto their path and were able to make the journey down the mountain successfully, with only a few minor cuts and bruises.

After crossing the cold and damp roads of the South Lowlands, they detected a noticeable dip in temperature. However, they didn't make much of it since they were just passing through. Finally, they came to the bitingly cold breezy coast of the Island of Monarchs, where the ships sailed to the Newlands. It was crowded and hectic. The family of five bought five one-way tickets. "Five tickets to the Newlands please" the father nervously said. The boat was packed with all sorts of different people. Everyone was squashed on the ship. It felt crowded. There were suitcases upon suitcases, as well as an assortment of displayed emotions that seemed to take the little extra space that was left.

After days of rough seas causing a bit of seasickness, the family safely arrived in the Newlands. Momentarily forgetting their grueling journey, they collectively breathed a sigh of relief.

The family found a place to call "home" in the Newlands. The girl's brothers were excited, the mother was reflective, and the father was hesitantly optimistic. But when the girl saw plants and trees that were not AT ALL like the ones from the Island of Monarchs, she cried bitterly. Fear encroached upon her little heart. Everything seemed so different. She thought to herself, "What if I can't make new friends? What if I feel the same loneliness as I did in the Northern Mountains?" Then she muttered a whisper to herself, "At least my friends from the Northern Mountains understood me a little. It wasn't that bad, was it?" It seemed like the girl was inconsolable for days. Her parents felt powerless because this move was supposed to help their little girl, not harm her.

After a week, she finally broke her silence and told her parents, "I'm okay with the adventure. I don't even mind losing things, but I'm sad that I've lost the only friends I've ever had. It took them so long to like me in the first place." Her parents reminded her of her special Twinkle - that it would eventually get bigger. And potentially, she could have lost all her tribal community since they didn't fully accept her with the Twinkle; or something even worse could have happened. Bitterness could have persuaded her to deny her Twinkle and demanded the Starlight to remove it forever.

But the girl loved her Twinkle and couldn't imagine her life without it. Even though it made her lonely at times, it provided a constant daily comfort. She intuitively knew she was unusual, but this was the first time she truly understood that she was different. And as much as she enjoyed feeling special, she feared being rejected by the people in the Newlands more.

A little time went by. So, with a touch more confidence, the girl decided to do her best and make new friends. She did what she had always done. She would go up to strangers and say, "Hi, will you be my friend?" But it was only when she tried to make new friends that she suddenly became self-conscious of her appearance. Only then did she fully realize she was slightly chubby and had a crooked smile. Unfortunately, these were not acceptable qualities in the Newlands, and not many people accepted her invitation of friendship. Even though she made a few friends in the Newlands, her fear of rejection drove down deeper still. Feeling sorry for herself, she concluded that she'd have to mostly live a life of loneliness. Her biggest fear would become a reality. Just at that self-defeating moment, she was distracted by a joyful noise that was coming from the forest behind her house. "Who lives there?" she wondered. Curiosity got the better of her, and she walked through the bushes and trees only to see a marvelous party with lots of dancing!

There was a sub-clan in the Newlands, called the "Colorful Feathery Clan." They were fun, vibrant, and full of life. Most of them lived in tents because they liked to move often. They wore big, colorful feathers to represent the colorful and exciting life they were determined to have. They almost looked like fairies at first, but they were just delightfully magical in a different way. As she observed them from afar, her Twinkle shined brightly into the crowd. She quickly realized what had happened and ducked, fearful that they would see her. A member of the Colorful Feathery Clan did she her and quickly approached her. He said, "We couldn't help but notice your Twinkle in your eye. We love people with Twinkles! Please, come and join our dance party!" "Wow!" she thought; it was always her striving to make friends. "Who are these welcoming, colorful feathery people?" she thought quietly to herself. With caution, she joined them. The party was fun and loud. It was so much fun that she quickly lost track of time and danced until her little legs couldn't take any more. She became best friends with this clan and forgot all about her "unacceptable" appearance.

Time past by quickly. Seasons came and went. The slightly chubby girl grew up and started to slowly slim down because of all the dancing she was doing. She spent most of her time with the Colorful Feathery Clan. In fact, she was with them so much that she learned to communicate in some of their special tweets. Because of the Colorful Feathery Clan was diverse and so welcoming, many sorts of people joined their parties. Even the small people-group over the bridge called the "Pleasantry Scarfs" joined their parties from time to time.

The girl found that the Pleasantry Scarfs people were incredibly friendly too. It was their mutual love for colors that bonded them with the Colorful Feathery Clan. However, the Pleasantry Scarfs spoke a completely different language and didn't quite believe in Twinkles the same way they did. The Pleasantry Scarfs believed in the Eternal Land, but they thought that the Twinkle came from the moonlight instead of the Starlight and that the Twinkle was earned not inherited. Either way, they had more in common than they did not. And because there was always a party, such subjects of conversation were rarely addressed in the joyous atmosphere.

For a season, the girl felt delightedly fulfilled because she had a variety of friends that added so much color to her life: a few friends from the Newlands, her best friends from the Colorful Feathery Clan, and a select few from the Pleasantry Scarfs people. She thought to herself, "What a gift! Certainly, the dangerous journey from the Northern Mountains was worth it all. My parents were right all along!"

Life seemed so grand and sunny for the girl. Like her parents said, it seemed that she was able to bring the warmth of the Northern Mountains to the Newlands. Remarkably, despite her hardships, her heart did not shrink and remained big and released lots of warmth. Her Twinkle was growing, and she was surrounded by equally warm hearts. She was learning new ways and fascinating ideas every day from her eclectic group of friends. She couldn't have been happier, and her love for dance magnified.

But with no warning at all, dark clouds quickly imposed into her sunny day. The loud sound of breaking thunder thud into her heart. She was robbed! Her precious family heirloom that her Grandmother gave her from the Northern Mountains was missing. The girl was distraught. But what was more shocking to her was that she found it had been stolen one of her dearest friends from the Colorful Feathery Clan, whom she trusted so much.

The pain of the betrayal was unbearable for the girl. With floods of tears running down her cheeks and the inability to take full long breaths, she nervously stuttered to her Colorful Feathery Clan friend, "Why would you do this to me? What did I do wrong to deserve such a thing? The heirloom is one of the most precious things I ever had; and I don't have much. It can never be replaced." Her feelings of confusion and pain made her instantly flashback to the pains of the memories of the Northern Mountains. A flash of pain ran through her entire body. She assumed it was her Twinkle's fault, like she always did. "Is this because you truly don't like my Twinkle after all? I knew it!" she cried. The girl tried but she couldn't possibly understand why her dearest friend would do such a thing.

Nervously, her friend responded in a shaky, timid voice. "I'm truly sorry. I knew it was wrong. I didn't plan on doing it. I just came to see you, but you weren't home. I saw that the door was ajar, so I crept in. When I went through the doors, my eyes locked on the shiny, blue necklace." The friend paused, seeing he wasn't getting through to her. So, he angrily blurted out in selfish defense, "Why did you just casually place it on the table in the first place if it's so invaluable!?"

Another awkward pause occurred as they painfully stared at each other. It was like you could almost hear the girl's heart actually breaking. After a few more moments, which seemed to be the most uncomfortable silence she'd ever experienced, the friend calmed down and continued to explain. In a much softer tone he said, "I needed money, and I knew I could sell it for good value. It was reckless of me, and only now I am thinking about the consequences. Honestly, I didn't really think about how much it would upset you. I didn't think it through at all." He then explained to the girl, "Even though robbery is not accepted in our clan, sadly, it is something to expect because it happens so often. So, I tend not to take stealing seriously. Again, I am so very sorry. Could you ever forgive me?" the friend said, staring deeply in the girl's eyes.

While the girl's friend spoke with sincerity, it brought minimal comfort to her and she couldn't forgive. She had never felt so mistreated. She experienced new, deeper feelings that she had never had to process before, and it devastated her in every way. As days slowly passed by, she mourned over her loss and tried to accept that her family heirloom was gone forever. Those days were long and painful.

The girl didn't want to lose her friends as well as her heirloom, but she felt uncomfortable about attending the parties anymore, and she slowly disconnected from the group. During this time, the girl stayed home with her family much more often. She asked her mother to retell stories of her childhood in the Northern Mountains. The stories were healing because it bought her comfort, and it would make her Twinkle shine again for a moment. She so desperately wished that retelling the stories would bring back her family heirloom, but it didn't -nothing could.

In a quiet moment, the girl reflected deeply about all the experiences and all the new friends that she had made since she arrived. She decided that she should be more united in the ways of the Newlands. After all, that was why the family moved there. She continued to lose her chubbiness and having her teeth straightened, she felt a little more confident to embrace the people of the Newlands.

The girl had a sincere desire to be more knowledgeable about the new land she lived in; she wanted to get involved; she wanted to make new friends. She inquired about many opportunities, and she started to learn the ways of the Newlanders – how they think, feel, and act. Surprisingly, even though the Island of Monarchs and the Newlands had the same language, hardly anything else was the same. She enjoyed the optimism that the Newlanders brought and their passion for new inventions. It was their positivity for the future that the Newlanders had that made her Twinkle shine bright again. For the first time, she could begin to see the possibility of a bright future for her in the Newlands. Rather than believing she could just survive in the Newlands; she became optimistic that she could thrive there!

Time had partially healed the girl's heart, but not entirely. Others around her tried to encourage her by saying "With time, you will heal." It was then when she realized that time does not have the power to heal all things, especially deep emotions. But she knew it was time to reconnect with her old friends of the Colorful Feathery Clan and Pleasantry Scarfs people. With much courage, she attended one of their vibrant parties again. She realized at that moment, how much she had missed them, and they had missed her too! She seemed to have reclaimed many of her friendships and had the best of all worlds.

While getting more comfortable with all the variety again, she realized that she had never invited them into her home before. It was always her venturing out to them, but she never was vulnerable enough to bring them to her. With resolution and attempted forgiveness in her heart, she held one of their parties in her home. The night was going strong. Everyone was having a good time. Her family from the Northern Mountains, her new friends from the Newlands, and her friends from the Colorful Feathery Clan and Pleasantry Scarfs were all present. The girl delighted in the sight to have such diversity under her roof; everyone was dancing. So much so, her Twinkle set off the disco ball in the most fun way!

As the night was wearing down, something unexpected happened. Her dearest friend from the Colorful Feathery Clan, who had earlier betrayed her, and another member of the Pleasantry Scarfs started getting rambunctious. They must have had too much punch! They began to play dangerous games by the fireplace. The girl nervously giggled and said, "Be careful friends, we wouldn't want anything to end our party too soon." Her friends were so wrapped up in their games that they didn't take much notice of her. And just as the girl had warned them, something dropped on the fireplace, and the house caught on fire.

"Fire, fire, fire!" everyone screamed. "Get out, everyone!" the girl cried. Everyone panicked and scrambled out of the house. The girl frantically tried to put out the fire, waving her hands in fury and dumping as much water as she could in the most pitiful way. It was too late. The recklessness of her friends caused destruction to her home. The house completely burned down to its foundations.

Rather than being naturally outraged, the girl reacted differently this time. She was extremely mad at herself. She murmured under her breath, "How could I have been so foolish to let people into my life? What's the point of having friends! Sure, people are fun for a time, but in the end, they just cause pain. It's better to live life alone no matter where you live."

In a deafening stillness, she slumped defeated onto the floor, surrounded by the sight and smell of ashes of her crumbled home. The ash was so thick, it covered everything, even her eyes. Her vision was challenged, and she suddenly realized that the most unfathomable thing happened: her Twinkle had faded. It seemed to be gone. The girl looked up to the open sky where her roof used to be and shouted, "This wasn't supposed to happen!" Her eyes wanted to cry, but it seemed like she had run out of tears. The fading of her Twinkle was caused by the thick scales that covered her eyes to start the healing process. Because she didn't know the scales were a part of her healing process, she lost hope in all people and even the Starlight who gave her the Twinkle. In her scaly eyes, everything seemed to be a complete loss.

By this time, everyone had gone. Only her parents and the oldest brother stayed to console her. But there was one person from the party that stayed behind. A person that the girl didn't recognize. Although, she might not have recognized her closest friend with her scaly eyes, she could see his silhouette through her clouded vision. "Were you here for the party?" she asked the male stranger. "Yes, I never miss an event!" he replied. "Well, did you have a nice time while the party was going good?" she asked. "Of course, but actually, I'm more of a post-party type of guy" he replied. The girl wondered what he was talking about, but she was too weak and blind to care. The stranger walked closer to her and continued talking, "It's awful what's happened to you." The girl didn't mind him talking because he was charming and as far as she could tell with her limited vision, he was quite handsome too. And for a moment, it was nice for her to focus on something pleasant instead of ashes. He continued the conversation: "You don't know me, but I've been watching from afar. I know what you need right now, and I can give it to you." "Really?" the girl replied, "I doubt that" she continued. The stranger replied, "I can give you your family heirloom back, the one you've been aching over. It is what you want, right? It will make you so happy to get it back, you'll dance like you've never danced before!" Water instantly filled her scaly eyes and her heart started beating out of her chest. She wondered how a stranger could know her deepest desires. Gullibly, she desperately wanted to believe that it was possible, so she continued to listen to the stranger. "Do you want your heirloom back?" he sweetly asked. "Yes. Please! How could you achieve such a thing?" she bawled. "Oh, it's easy, I just need to ...." he looked away and paused. "You just need to what?" cried the girl. "I'm sorry, I'll be right back!" the stranger said.

Anxiously, she could make out that he was approaching a small boy who was passing by. The girl was hanging on by a thread, so she eavesdropped to see what was so important that he had to leave mid-sentence. "Hey, young lad" he said to the small boy who was passing by, "I heard that your birthday party was cancelled, and you couldn't wait to have balloons at your party. You know, I can give you a thousand balloons!" He pulled one out from his pocket, but it had a tiny hole in it. He blew it up and give it to the small boy, and it instantly deflated. The stranger's eyes turned from pleasant to nasty within a second as he whispered something evil to the young boy. The boy almost obeyed the stranger's instruction, but the boy's mother came out of nowhere and grabbed the little boy's arm and pulled him away from danger.

The girl was horrified at this strange and unknown man. "Who are you, really? I demand answers!" In aggravation, he sternly replied, "My name is Bitterness. I like to hang out at tragic events. I watch everyone very very closely. After a tragedy has taken place, I like to pretend that I can offer the person's deepest desire, but I can never, ever deliver. If the tragedy doesn't finish you off, I make sure I will." He cruelly sniggered, "You know, some people confuse me with Justice. Isn't that funny?" But then he scoffed under his breath with what seemed to be jealousy - "But only the Starlight can do that. Why does he have to take all the credit, huh?" Stunned by his very honest reply, she stuttered, "Wow, but, but, but, but you looked so nice and made me feel right for grieving my losses and wanting justice. How can that be?" He replied, "If I showed you who I really was, you would never entertain me, and that's damaging to my business, silly girl." The girl did feel silly that she was momentarily attracted to this evil man. "Well, I don't want any of your business here, Bitterness. I need real Justice, not pretend justice that leaves me deflated like that boy's balloon. Leave me alone and get out of what remains of my house!" she confidently shouted. Bitterness left, but before he did, he reminded her that she will see him at every tragic event in her future, and that she'll never forget his face.

It was the middle of the night by now, and sheer exhaustion finally put her to sleep. The Starlight came to her in a dream, the very Starlight that had visited her father in the Northern Mountains. The Starlight gently said, "Hello, my dear sunshine. Why are you so downcast and troubled?" In shock and almost in complete disbelief that the Starlight couldn't see what just happened to her, she replied with what seemed to be all in one breath, "Can't you see the state of my house? Don't you know what I've lost: my hometown, my family heirloom, my friends, and now my new home?" She paused because she was breathing so hard. She wanted to angrily continue to tell the Starlight her disdain for her current situation, but she wasn't brave enough to to say anything more out loud. However, she thought to herself, "Did the smoke blur the Starlight sight too? Ugh!" Even though she didn't say anything more, the Starlight knew what she was thinking. (For the Starlight always knows what people are thinking.) The Starlight knew her pain and understood her disappointment more than she could ever possibly realize. With love and compassion, the Starlight approached her closer, and asked, "Do you want your eyes to be healed, my darling sunshine?" She responded in a doubtful tone, "I don't know if healing is even possible." She shyly continued, "Starlight, why do people hurt me and why does the Twinkle reject me from others? I'm just a girl from the Northern Mountains who wants to fit in. I don't want this trouble in my life. It's too hard. I can't cope anymore. I want to experience the goodness of having the Twinkle, not the struggle; just like I used to believe when I was a very little girl." The Starlight responded, "The reward of sharing in the Starlight's goodness comes to those who are also willing to share in the struggle of loving others." At that point, she achingly realized that all this time, she had always been more concerned about who liked her or who hurt more than the Starlight who made her special in the first place.

The Starlight continued, "My darling sunshine, you've looked at your Twinkle the wrong way. It's not there to separate you from people. It was given to you so you can have the power to love all people, just the way I do. You've been so doubtful about your Twinkle, that you have lowered the value of yourself before any person could ever accept you. You've always assumed that you'll be rejected because they don't understand the Twinkle. The reality my darling sunshine - it's you who doesn't fully understand the gift of the Twinkle. People are people and are very capable of mistakes. They can love and hurt you all in the same day, even the same hour. More often than not, people make mistakes that affect you because of their own personal issues, not because they have chosen to hurt you. In fact, you are also capable of hurting people when you are in pain. It's just that the pain has made you so short-sighted that you cannot see the effect that you extend onto others. So, let me ask you again, my darling sunshine, do you want your eyes healed? Do you want your Twinkle restored? If you do, I am willing to heal you. However, I must ask you for two things: First, to forgive all those who have hurt you in their unawareness of their own struggles. Second, I need you to accept yourself for who you are; a girl from the Northern Mountains whom the Starlight loves and has gifted with a Twinkle." The girl pondered in silence for a while. She knew she wanted to be healed, but she didn't know if she wanted to forgive everyone who had hurt her (it was a long list) and she always had struggled with accepting herself. She was so used to living with a lingering, nagging feeling of embarrassment of her true self and had experienced the reality of not fitting in anywhere for so long that she didn't know how to think of herself in any other way than being less than. A few moments went by; flashes of more painful memories invaded her mind – of betrayal, loneliness, and extreme disappointment. Her breaths got shorter, her hands started to nervously shake, and she got goosebumps over her entire body because of cold chills from just dwelling on the past memories. She finally responded with a timid, shaky voice, "Starlight, please help me to forgive others and accept myself. I can't live like this anymore."

Just at that moment, a beam of light came bursting forth, and it peeled back the scales from her eyes. The Starlight give her a final remark before she woke up: "My darling sunshine, I don't want you to fear people anymore or the bad news they unknowingly carry with them. Please know that with everything that happens to you in the future, I will make sure it turns out for your good because you are well loved, and you belong to Me." The girl awoke from her dream. The scales did indeed drop off, and her Twinkle was more significant and brighter than ever before!

The girl understood that her circumstances didn't have to change in order to have a happier life, but her perspective did. From that day she vowed that she would always accept herself, even when she perceived that others didn't. She also had the confidence that she could face any bad news because the Starlight will always be there for her. With that vow, the decision to always dance, even if her dance partners leave her, was strengthened in her mind.

Bravely, she reengaged with her multi-cultural friends. Even though she didn't expect them to be any different, she was pleasantly surprised when her friend who stole her family heirloom worked all night to make her a new necklace to replace the one that was stolen. The new necklace was beautifully thought out. It was inspired by the old heirloom that she had lost, but with the addition of feathers and pieces of scarfs symbolizing all the experiences that had made her to a more complete person.

In the end, she learned that everyone had the power to hurt her: from her own tribe to her new culture and the sub-cultures therein. However, after understanding the Love that the Starlight provides, she discovered a greater power to love others, despite her vulnerabilities. The girl doesn't fully know where her Twinkle will take her in the future, but she knows it has given her the power to love and accept all people (even herself) and that is something to dance about!

The End.

It usually takes a deep journey in God for a person to feel secure in their identity while also accepting others as they are. In *The Girl from the Northern Mountains,* we meet a young girl who embarks on that journey. Set apart from her native people by the Twinkle that she inherited from the Eternal Starlight, The Girl grows up knowing that she is different. When her family makes the decision to leave the Northern Mountains where she was born and travel to the Newlands, the Twinkle goes with her, even as all she knew about herself and the world gets left behind. A story about the desire to belong and the deep need we all have to embrace forgiveness as we accept people, *The Girl from the Northern Mountains* is for anyone who has ever wondered who they are and where they fit in. It's a story for all of us!

 Lois Furtado was born and raised in a ministry home in the North-East of England. Their family's ministry led them to immigrate to South Florida when Lois was a teenager. Lois remembers giving her life to Christ at a tender age of five and was internally challenged to keep her faith even when it wasn't popular to do so. Lois still resides in multi-cultural South Florida with her Brazilian husband and two children. Lois earned her Master of Science in Organizational Leadership, achieved her Ordination to serve as a local children's pastor, and currently works for a global children's ministry.

Printed in the United States
By Bookmasters